The Cardinal's Gift

A True Story of Finding Hope in Grief

CAROLE HEANEY

Illustrated by **MARLO GARNSWORTHY**

To my husband, Tom R., friends Kate Coss and Judith Spross, thank you for planting and nurturing the seed to bring this book to life.

To my older grandchildren, Jack, Noah, Caspar, and Mia, your honesty and love kept my inspiration alive.

To cardinal lovers everywhere, continue to be divinely inspired by our feathered friends.

IN THE SPIRIT OF
Healing Press
www.healingpress.net

Published by In the Spirit of Healing Press

Library of Congress Control Number: 2021923983

Paperback ISBN: 978-1-7367755-0-9
Hardcover ISBN: 978-1-7367755-1-6

Written by Carole Heaney
Illustration and cover design by Marlo Garnsworthy
Interior design by Misty Black Media, LLC

First Edition 2021

For Kelly and Michael,

In memory of Dad, who lives forever in our hearts.

Love, Mom

"Rachel, please get ready for school," Mom called. "If you don't get up, you'll miss the bus."

Ever since Daddy died, Rachel didn't want to get up in the morning, let alone go to school. Reading her favorite books or watching TV was hard. At times, she didn't even want to play with her friends. Her thoughts were so confused.

School wasn't much better. Rachel never knew what to say to her friends. They tried to cheer her up, but it was no use.

She just stared out the window waiting until she could go home and curl up under her quilt again.

The next morning, Rachel huddled under her quilt, dreading Mom's call. She loved this cozy space. She could remember more about Daddy—things she was afraid she would forget.

As she lay there, a tapping came from the window. She pulled her pillow over her head, but the sound grew louder.

TAP, TAP, TAP!

"Go away," Rachel groaned.

When the tapping continued, Rachel threw off her blankets and stomped to the window. "What?" she shouted when she saw a cardinal banging its beak against the glass.

Rachel pressed her fingers to the window. Daddy had loved cardinals. He called them fire in the sky. The cold seeped through the glass, chilling Rachel's hand, and she shook her head. "Go away, noisy bird," she said, and knocked hard on the glass. Startled, the cardinal flew away.

Late again, Rachel rushed into the bathroom to wash her face.

Tap, tap, tap came from the window.

Confused, Rachel pulled back the curtain and could not believe her eyes. The bathroom window was on the other side of the house from her bedroom.

"How did he get here so fast?" Rachel wondered as he danced in the window. She banged on the glass, and off he went.

"Rachel, the bus is HERE!" cried Mom.

The next morning, a loud TAP, TAP, TAP, woke Rachel.

Curious, she marched to the window. Sure enough, there was the cardinal again, pecking so hard he left marks on the glass.

Rachel sighed. What is wrong with this bird? she wondered, looking at the cardinal.

The bird stared back, directly into Rachel's eyes. "Ugh, shoo-shoo!" Rachel cried, tapping on the glass.

She was up now, so she dressed and trudged downstairs.

Rachel awoke the next day to the same loud pecking by the cardinal on the glass. "This bird made a better alarm than my clock," she thought.

At school, Rachel got distracted imagining why the cardinal might be visiting her.

Rachel told her mom about the curious morning visits from her feathered friend. "Do you think the cardinal is hungry?" she asked. "Should we feed him? Why is he coming to my window?"

"Did you know cardinal visits have many meanings?" said Mom. "For some, it's a heavenly reminder of a loved one who has died. For others, it's a sign of love, luck, or hope when we are worried or sad."

"But just in case, let's put the feeder out," Mom said.

Each morning the cardinal returned to Rachel's window. She never saw him at the feeder.

Mom thought he was protecting a nest nearby.

One thing was for sure, Rachel got excited whenever he arrived. Even if only for a moment, it made her feel better.

Rachel began sitting up in bed, watching the window closely for her new friend to arrive. When he did, she made a wish.

She heard the melody of his song—*cheer-cheer, twill-twill*—long before he arrived. *I'm awake before my friend.*

Rachel looked forward to seeing the cardinal in the mornings and was hopeful she would see him every morning.

Hopeful to see the cardinal each day, Rachel woke before he arrived. She continued to be surprised when he appeared.

Then one day, Rachel realized she'd been waking and dressing before the visit from her feathered friend. She had time for breakfast and wasn't late for the bus.

It's like he's cheering me on to a new day... a better day.

Finally, summer arrived. Even though Rachel could sleep late now, she didn't. She was up with the birds.

As the summer went on, Rachel took more interest in playing with her friends.

She laughed more.

She shared her feelings with other kids who had lost a parent. Most of the time these things helped Rachel feel better.

Fall had arrived, and Rachel found herself missing her Daddy so much. "Mom, how do you make the hurt stop?"

"Missing someone can make your heart ache, Rachel," Mom said. "It's because you love Daddy so much. It might not take the hurt away, but you can do things to remind yourself what you love and miss about him. You can always talk to me or call a friend or Nona. Looking at our family pictures might comfort you, too.

Rachel found treasured pictures and reminders of Daddy and filled his favorite box with them. She glued her cardinal drawing on the top and created a memory box so she wouldn't forget.

Soon winter arrived, and Rachel's mood changed with it. She wondered how she and Mommy could have a merry Christmas without Daddy. Just the thought made her sad. She'd hoped to see her cardinal friend to cheer her up.

But on Christmas morning . . .

. . . Rachel opened a special gift. "Mom, I love it! My very own cardinal". She watched the snowflakes falling around his red feathers.

Her tears stung as she remembered those spring mornings when she couldn't get out of bed. That is when the cardinal appeared at her window.

"The cardinal visits came at just the right time," said Rachel, "and now, I have a cardinal to greet me every day."

When Rachel and Mom remembered things about Daddy, they laughed and cried.

"Sometimes I miss Daddy more when we talk about him, but it feels good to remember," Rachel said.

Mom hugged her. "That's okay, Rachel. Our memories remind us Daddy has a forever home in our hearts. It's like our very own Daddy hug."

The cardinal reminded Rachel of Daddy's love, giving her hope and encouragement.

And now she knew . . .

Mother Nature's special gift would live forever in her heart.

Author's Message

When someone dies, we miss being near them so much, it hurts. Our emotions may change from sadness, anger, fear, and joy within moments. Grief is those feelings, and more. It feels confusing, but all feelings are okay.

Sharing with family, friends, teachers, or counselors we trust can help us understand our grief, as is writing, drawing, music, playing, and spending time in nature.

Mother Nature gave us birds, trees, butterflies, clouds, and rainbows to bring us comfort and encouragement. The cardinal became my gift as I grieved. His visits still give me hope. They remind us love does not leave us when someone dies. Instead, it finds a forever home in our hearts.

That is when I say a little prayer and make a wish.

About the Author

Carole Heaney is a mom, nona, wife, nurse, end-of-life doula, grief coach, and author. Her nursing background in hospice care and personal experience with death and dying encouraged her to share this story which brought great comfort to her following a family death.

Writing this book led to sharing memories with her grandchildren about a grandad they will never meet while creating a forever place in their hearts and deepening their understanding of how grief keeps love alive.

To share your cardinal story and for additional resources, visit healingpress.net.

IN THE SPIRIT OF
Healing Press
www.healingpress.net

Made in the USA
Las Vegas, NV
31 October 2023

79923273R00021